David
McPhail

Voyager Books
Harcourt, Inc.

ORLANDO   AUSTIN   NEW YORK   SAN DIEGO   TORONTO   LONDON

www.HarcourtBooks.com

First Voyager Books edition 2006

Voyager Books is a trademark of Harcourt, Inc., registered in the United States of America and/or other jurisdictions.

The Library of Congress has cataloged the hardcover edition as follows:
McPhail, David, 1940–
Big Brown Bear's up and down day/written and illustrated by David McPhail.
p. cm.
Summary: Big Brown Bear is visited by a rat who wants to use one of his slippers for a bed.
[1. Bears—Fiction. 2. Rats—Fiction.] I. Title.
PZ7.M2427Bh 2003
[E]—dc21   2002015854
ISBN-13: 978-0152-16407-2   ISBN-10: 0-15-216407-3
ISBN-13: 978-0152-05684-1 pb   ISBN-10: 0-15-205684-X pb

H G F E D C B A

Big Brown Bear's
Up and
Down
Day

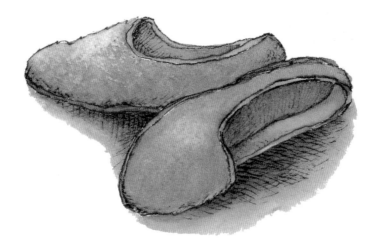

Big Brown Bear's Up and Down Day

For John, who made Big Brown Bear shine.

—D. M.

One

Big Brown Bear woke up and opened his eyes. He rolled over, and when he looked down, he saw one of his slippers scooting across the floor.

"Stop, slipper!" yelled Big Brown Bear. The slipper stopped moving, and a head poked out from beneath it. It looked like a mouse.

"Hey, mouse," growled Big Brown Bear. "Where are you going with that slipper?"

"I'm not a mouse," said the slipper thief. "I'm a rat, and I'm taking this slipper home. It will make a good bed for me to sleep in."

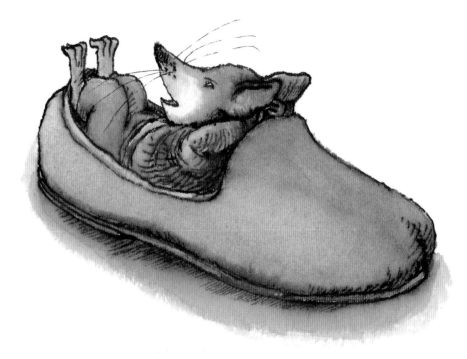

"Well, Rat," said Big Brown Bear, "it may make a good bed, but it makes a better slipper. Now put it back!"

"But you have two of them," said Rat.

Two

Big Brown Bear put on his slippers and
then went downstairs to the kitchen.

Further argument would be useless—
Rat could see *that*. So he abandoned the
slipper, and disappeared through a hole
in the wall.

Big Brown Bear swung his feet over the side of the bed and slammed them down hard on the floor.

"I have two feet, too," he said to Rat.
"And two feet need two slippers."

There he cooked up a big pot of oatmeal.

While the oatmeal was cooking, he got a bowl down from the cupboard.

He filled up a pitcher with cream and set it down on the kitchen table.

He was standing at the stove, stirring the oatmeal, when the doorbell rang.

Who could that be? wondered Big Brown Bear. *Our baseball game isn't until this afternoon.*

When Big Brown Bear went to the door and opened it, no one was there.

At least he didn't see anybody—until he looked down.
Even then all he could see was the top of a wide-brimmed
hat with a long nose sticking out from under the brim.

Big Brown Bear leaned down. There was a rat under that hat—the very same rat that had been trying to steal his slipper.

"What do you want now?" Big Brown Bear asked. "As you can see, I'm wearing my slippers, so don't expect me to give you one."

"I don't want anything from you," explained Rat. "Instead, I have something for you." He put down the satchel he was carrying and opened it up. "You have won a trip," said Rat, "and I'm here to present it to you."

"What sort of trip?" asked Big Brown Bear.

"Any sort of trip you want," answered Rat. "Up to the mountains, or down to the seashore. Up to the North Pole, or down to the South Pole."

"What it sounds like," said Big Brown Bear, "is an up or down sort of trip."

"It's all up to you," said Rat. "Now let's get down to the business of deciding where you'll be going."

Big Brown Bear began to pace up and down the walk. When he came to where Rat was standing, he bent down and said, "Hmmmm . . . how soon can I go on this trip?"

"Right away," said Rat. "But you can't wear your slippers. They're not allowed on this trip. Says so right here in the fine print." And he took some papers out of his satchel and held them up in front of Big Brown Bear's nose.

"No slippers?" asked Big Brown Bear. "What an odd rule that is. But I suppose I can pack them in my suitcase."

"I'm afraid not," said Rat. "That's rule number forty-seven. No slippers allowed in suitcases."

Finally, Big Brown Bear stopped pacing and sat down to pull his slippers on tighter.

"I've decided where I want to go," he told Rat.

"Where?" asked Rat.

"Nowhere!" said Big Brown Bear. "Not up, not down. I want to stay right here!"

Rat slowly put the papers back in his satchel and started to walk away.

"How about a nice bowl of oatmeal before you go?" asked Big Brown Bear.

"That would be good," said Rat.

"I'm starving."

Big Brown Bear led the way to his kitchen. He got down another bowl and filled up both bowls with oatmeal. He sliced some bananas and placed them on top.

Rat grabbed a spoon and started in. He didn't put down the spoon until the bowl was scraped clean. "I'm filled up!" he said to Big Brown Bear. "Thank you, that was delicious!"

Then he waddled to a hole in the kitchen wall and squeezed through.

"You're most welcome," Big Brown Bear called after him. But not before he looked down to make sure he still had both slippers on.

Three

Big Brown Bear went to find his baseball and mitt. He found them on a shelf in his closet.

As he was getting them down, the baseball fell into a big box.

The box was filled with all sorts of things that he hadn't seen in a long time.

On top was his old yellow windup racing car.

Big Brown Bear wound up the key, then put the car down on the floor. ZOOM! Away it went.

"Still works," said Big Brown Bear.

Next, he pulled out his old maroon sweater with the gold
B on the front.

He tugged it down over his head and tried it on.

"It has a few moth holes," he said, "but it still fits!"

Big Brown Bear was taking something else out of the box when he heard his car coming back. And Rat was driving!

"What a wonderful car!" said Rat. "Wherever did you find it?"

"I found it in this box full of old stuff," Big Brown Bear said, "while I was looking for my baseball."

"I will help you look for your ball," said Rat. "I am small, and I can see in the dark."

He climbed into the box to help Big Brown Bear find his baseball.

Big Brown Bear found his old cowboy hat and plopped it down on his head. "I can wear this while I play ball," he said.

He reached into the box one more time and came up with
a well-worn slipper, just as Rat popped up holding the
missing baseball.

"I found it!" shouted Rat.

"Good job!" said Big Brown Bear. "And I found something for you!"

"It will make a perfect bed!" Rat said. "Thank you."

"You're welcome," said Big Brown Bear. "And there's something else I want you to have, too."

He wound up the windup car and held it steady while Rat loaded the slipper into the back and then jumped in front behind the wheel.

When Big Brown Bear let it go, the car sped away.

"Yippee!" yelled the rat. "So long, Bear!"
"So long to you, too, Rat!"

Then Big Brown Bear picked up his ball and mitt and went outside to play.

The illustrations in this book were done in pen and ink and watercolor.
The display type and text type were set in Old Claude.
Color separations by Bright Arts Ltd., Hong Kong
Printed and bound by Tien Wah Press, Singapore
Production supervision by Ginger Boyer
Designed by Suzanne Fridley